Sticker Life Stories

Marie Curie

Written by Evie Daye
Illustrated by Ana Sanfelippo

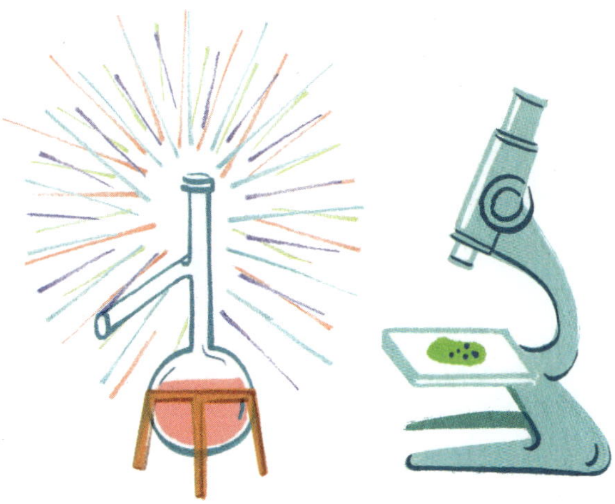

MAGIC CAT PUBLISHING

A brilliant daughter

Marie Curie wanted to be a scientist since she was a little girl – even though she grew up in a time when it was nearly impossible for women to do so. She was born Maria Salomea Skłodowska on 7 November 1867, in Warsaw, Poland.

Marie's mother and one of her older sisters, Zofia, died when Marie was very young. Her father was a maths and science teacher.

Marie's father worked hard to raise his children to love learning. All of her other older siblings – Józef, Bronisława and Helena – grew up to become scientists or teachers.

Marie was very clever, with an incredible memory. She won many academic awards, including a gold medal.

Star student in Paris

Even though Marie was very bright, in Poland only men were allowed to go to university. So Marie saved up money and moved to Paris to study maths and science at a famous university called the Sorbonne.

The Eiffel Tower was a new building when Marie moved to the city.

Sorbonne University

Marie didn't have much experience speaking French before moving to Paris, and her classes were very challenging. But she worked hard, studying day and night.

Her hard work paid off! When she graduated, Marie was first in her class in physics and second in mathematical sciences. Now, it was time to find a laboratory!

Marie often wore all the clothes she owned at once to keep warm in her little flat.

To avoid interrupting her studies, Marie often ate quick meals of just bread, butter and tea.

Partners in the lab, and in life

Marie searched all over Paris to find the perfect lab to do her scientific research in. Eventually, she found one that was run by a man named Pierre Curie.

Pierre was a well-known physicist and professor at the School of Industrial Physics and Chemistry.

Marie and Pierre met and began to work together in 1894. They realized that they had a lot in common: both their fathers were teachers and they both had taken unconventional paths to their jobs.

They were both very passionate and hopeful about their work.

The two quickly realized that they worked well together – and fell in love. They were married in 1895.

Pierre encouraged Marie to get her teacher's diploma so that she could teach students about all the work that they were doing.

Radiation detective

Even though Marie's laboratory was often crowded, and she spent many hours teaching on top of doing experiments, she wouldn't let anything stop her from her research. She was fascinated by a concept that's now known as radiation.

Everything on Earth is made up of atoms. Atoms contain different smaller particles called protons, neutrons and electrons.

Different numbers of protons, neutrons and electrons can be combined to make elements – which are substances like gold or oxygen or sodium.

Some elements are radioactive. This means that the element releases energy.

Radioactivity was officially discovered by a scientist named Henri Becquerel in 1896, but he was inspired by the research that the Curies were doing.

Marie believed that the element uranium was radioactive, and she did tests to prove it!

Elemental innovator

In their research, the Curies actually discovered two new elements: polonium and radium. These are elements that we previously didn't know existed in the world.

Marie named polonium after Poland, where she was born.

Radium is poisonous when eaten and can also cause some kinds of cancers, so it's not used very much for everyday things anymore.

Once scientists learned about the new elements, they could use them for all sorts of things.

Po

28

Polonium can be used as a heat source for space equipment.

Static eliminator brush

It can also prevent static build-up (which causes static shocks).

Ra

29

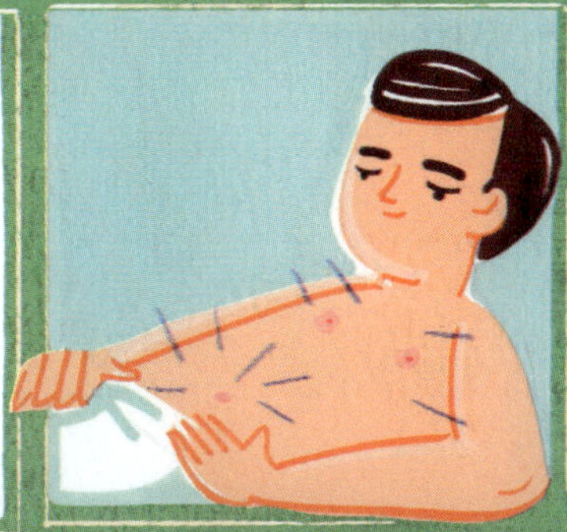

Radium was previously used to treat tumours.

It was also once used to create the glow on clock dials.

Polonium and radium occur naturally in the Earth in very small amounts. The Curies found them in a mineral called pitchblende.

30

In their natural states, polonium and radium look metallic. Polonium is a silvery grey metal and radium is a silvery white metal.

Pioneering prizewinner

Marie and Pierre won the Nobel Prize in Physics in 1903 for their revolutionary research. They were the first married couple to win the prize.

Marie was the first woman to ever win the prize!

At the same time, Marie was also awarded a prize from the Royal Society, as well as a doctorate degree for her work. She was the first woman to receive a Doctor of Science degree in France.

Even though Marie grew up being told she couldn't be a scientist because she was a girl, she proved people wrong time and time again – beating every expectation that the world had for her.

Marie may have been the first woman to win a Nobel Prize for Physics – but she wasn't the last!

Working mother

Marie and Pierre welcomed their first daughter, Irène, into their family in 1897. Seven years later, in 1904, their second daughter, Eve, was born.

Then, on 19 April 1906, Marie's world changed forever. Pierre was in a terrible accident and died.

Even though the loss of her husband was incredibly difficult, Marie maintained their lab, continued their research and looked after their children – all on her own.

After Pierre's death, Marie took over his role as Professor of General Physics at the Sorbonne.

Marie was the first woman to teach at the Sorbonne.

Remarkable researcher

In 1909, after many years of work, Marie was given her own research lab in Paris. Like many scientists, she used what's called the scientific method when doing her experiments, which has six steps.

1. OBSERVE
Marie would pay attention to the world around her and find something that she didn't yet understand to take a closer look at.

2. RESEARCH
She would read the work of other scientists to learn more about the topic she was exploring and what other scientists had done in the past.

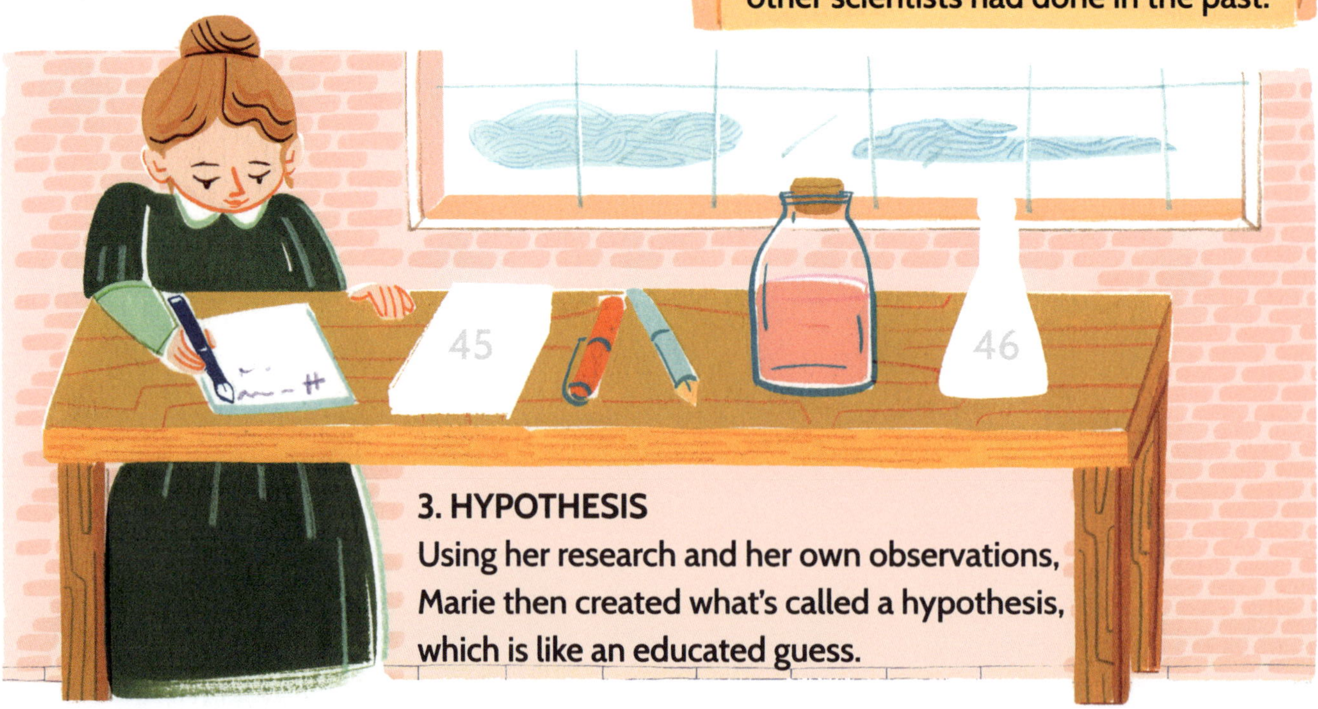

3. HYPOTHESIS
Using her research and her own observations, Marie then created what's called a hypothesis, which is like an educated guess.

4. EXPERIMENT

Next, Marie had to test her hypothesis to see if she was right. She had to do an experiment again and again to collect data to help her figure out answers.

5. ANALYSE

Once she'd collected data, Marie had to look over all her results. Sometimes, she had to do some maths to help her better understand the research she had done.

6. CONCLUSIONS

The data helped Marie to figure out some answers to her original question. She then shared what she'd found with other scientists, so that they could use her findings in their research for future experiments.

Hardworking academic

At her new lab, Marie worked harder than ever. In 1911, she won a second Nobel Prize – this time for Chemistry. She was the first person to win two Nobel Prizes.

Radiation became a key part of medicine.

Marie won the second Nobel for her research in isolating pure radium.

Between 1901 and 2023, only sixty-four women have won the Nobel Prize, and only four people so far have won two Nobel Prizes.

In 1911, Marie also became a member of the Conseil de Physique Solvay (a very important group of scientists) and was appointed to be the Director of Curie Labs in the Radium Institute of the University of Paris.

Marie is still the only woman to win the Nobel Prize for two different fields.

The discoveries Marie made were useful in other areas of science. Knowledge of radiation even helped scientists measure the age of Earth more accurately.

Humanitarian and hero

In 1914, World War I broke out – and Marie's scientific findings were once more put to good use.

Marie had been developing and improving X-rays, which helped doctors to see broken bones or bullet wounds inside a soldier's body.

Marie's daughter, Irène, worked closely alongside her to help care for the soldiers.

With a picture of the injury, doctors could take better care of the wounded soldiers.

Marie created mobile X-ray units. These machines became known as Little Curies, and they could be driven directly onto the battlefield so soldiers could be tended to quickly.

Marie became the Director at the Red Cross Radiology Service, and her Little Curies saved the lives of more than a million soldiers!

Leaving a legacy

Marie was a revolutionary scientific figure who wasn't afraid to defy expectations of what women should be or what they could do.

In 1921, Marie travelled to the United States and received a gram of radium from President Warren G. Harding, in thanks for the work she'd done.

Marie is an important part of the history of Sorbonne University.

When the war ended in 1918, many young women went to Paris to study science, having been inspired by Marie.

Later in her life, Marie was also elected to serve on the League of Nations and travelled with her daughters to give lectures. She died on 4 July 1934, of aplastic anemia – a side effect of being exposed to so much radiation.

Marie lives on through her legacy.
She helped to advance nuclear physics,
engineering and biology.

Her work has changed and saved the
lives of so many people, epecially
through its use in cancer research.

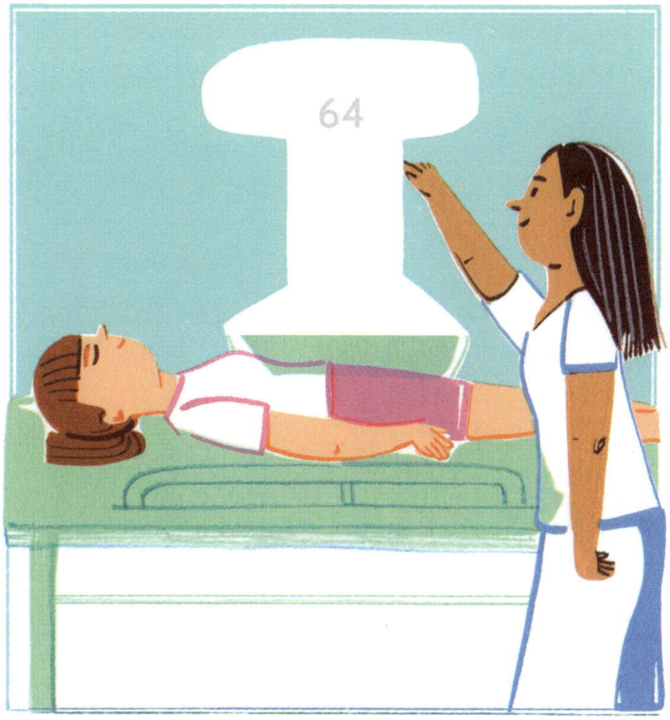

Marie's own daughter was even inspired by
her to become a scientist. Irène won a
Nobel Prize in Chemistry, just like her
mother did.

Marie Curie was an inspiration to so many,
and her work and life are proof of the
limitless possibilities of what we can do
when we set our mind to it!

Experiment like Marie!

Marie Curie was a brilliant scientist who conducted many different experiments. You can do an experiment of your own with oil and water. Use the stickers to complete the instructions and then try it in real life, with help from a grown-up.

1. Fill a jar about a third full with water.

2. Add a few drops of food colouring to the water. Does the colour mix with the water?

3. Then, add roughly 60 ml of vegetable oil to the jar. Does it mix with the water?

4. Shake the jar. What happens when you do?

5. What happens next? Observe the jar for a few minutes and record your findings.

Why does the oil always sit on top of the water? Can you do some research to find out?

Use the numbers to find the right place for each sticker in the story...

22

33

21

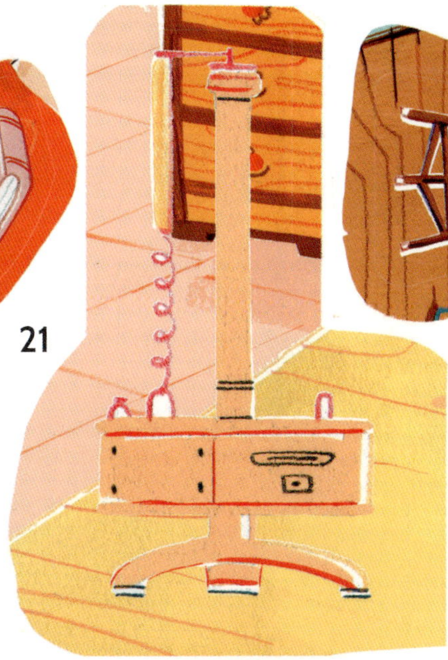

27

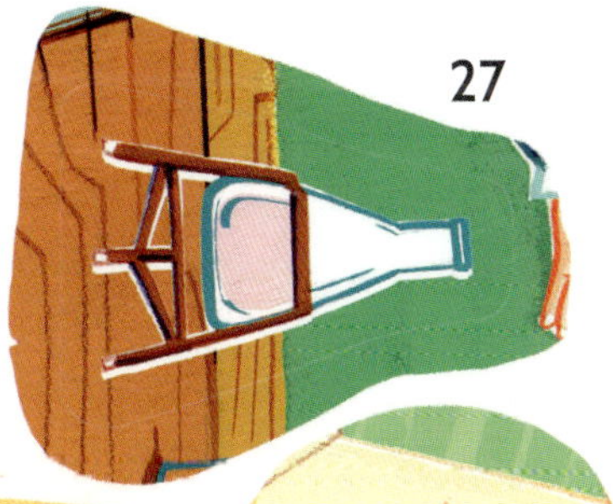

19

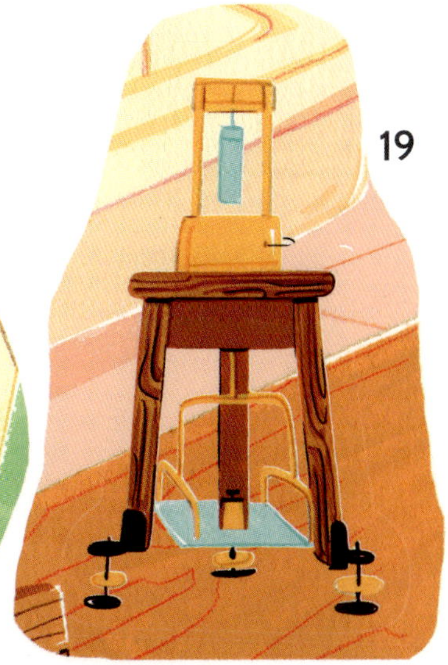

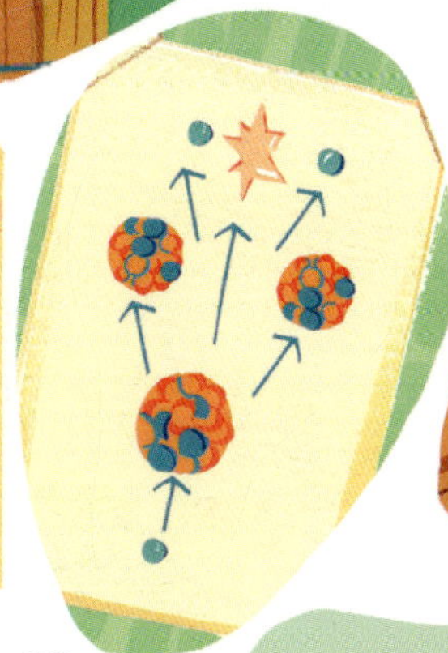

23

26

35

20

25

32

36

31

30

34

28

29

24

37

38

39

40

50

49

43

41

45

46

42

55

47

48

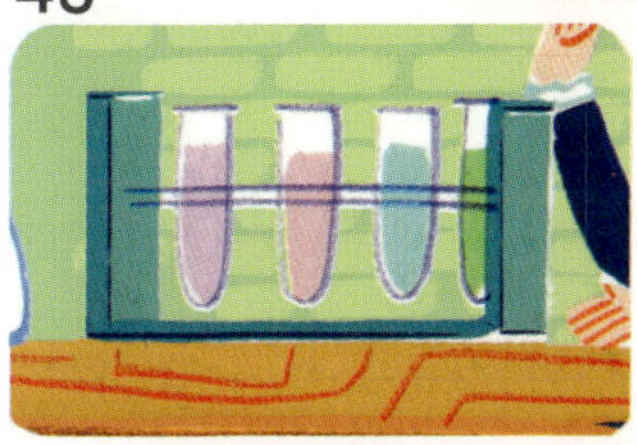

44

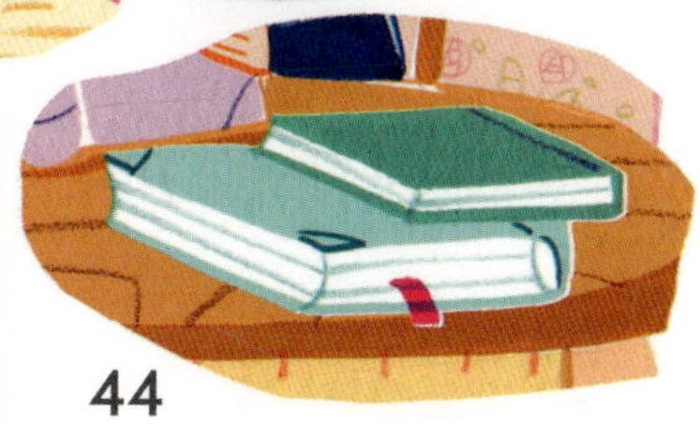

52

51

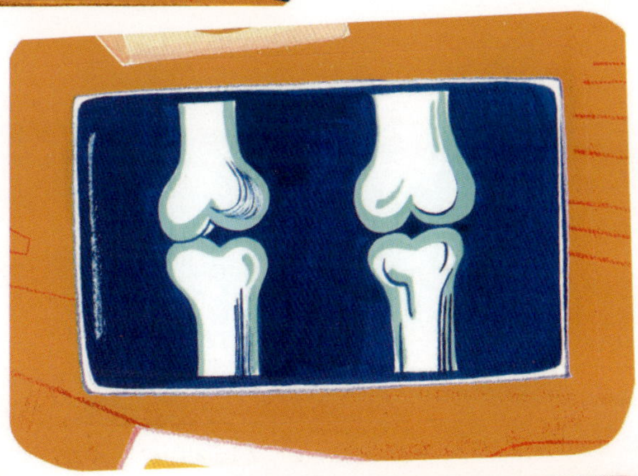

54

53

57
56
70
65
62
64
63
58
66
60
59
67
69
71
61
68